Whose Turtle?

THE WORLD PUBLISHING COMPANY

CLEVELAND AND NEW YORK

Whose Turtle?

DORIS ORGEL

Illustrations by Martha Alexander

Published by the World Publishing Company
2231 West 110th Street, Cleveland, Ohio 44102
Published simultaneously in Canada by
Nelson, Foster & Scott Ltd.
Library of Congress catalogue card number: 68-14683
Text copyright © 1968 Doris Orgel
Illustrations copyright © 1968 Martha Alexander
Printed in the United States of America.

Whose Turtle?

"Jump!" said Wally.

Rachel and he stood on an old three-sided wall at the far end of a wide brambly field. This had always been Wally and his friend Buddy's favorite hide-out. But Buddy had moved away, and now Wally had let his sister come.

Rachel hesitated. The wall was higher than she.

"Go on!"

She closed her eyes and jumped.

"Now watch me!" said Wally.

He landed way beyond her. But he stayed crouched on all fours, perfectly still. Why didn't he get up and shout that he had won the jumping contest?

Suddenly his arm lunged out. He snatched something off the ground. "Look what I found!" he yelled, holding up his prize.

It was a turtle, a beautiful big one.

Rachel ran to see it from close. Its shell was dark, almost black, with a pattern of yellow spots. Its feet clawed the air. Its head was hidden inside the shell.

"You should have heard him hiss when I grabbed him," said Wally. "Box turtles do that when they're scared." He knew, because he had read lots of books about animals. "Don't be scared," he told the box turtle. "Take your head out. I'm not going to hurt you, Buddy."

"Buddy? How do you know it's a boy?" asked Rachel.

"I saw his eyes and they're red. Only male turtles have red eyes. Females have yellow, or gray, or brown ones."

The turtle drew his head out a tiny bit.

"That's a good Buddy-boy!" said Wally.

"How old do you suppose he is?" asked Rachel.

Wally tapped on Buddy's shell. "It's hard," he said. "And he's at least six inches long. That means he's grown-up. He could be anywhere from six to a hundred years old. Turtles get pretty old, you know."

"Can I hold him?" asked Rachel.

"Okay, but just for a minute."

The turtle's feet still clawed the air. Rachel had to hold on to him with both hands. "Listen, Wally," she said, "you already have a hamster, and two toads, and a salamander. All I have is a goldfish. I'll give you my goldfish, if you'll—"

"Finders, keepers," said Wally and took Buddy back. "Come on, let's get him home."

There was an old wooden washtub in the basement that nobody used. "I'll keep Buddy in there," said Wally.

Rachel was surprised. "Why don't you keep him in a box?" she asked.

"You mean because he's a box turtle?" That made Wally laugh. "Look," he said, and he showed her Buddy's underside. "See that crack across the middle? It works like a hinge, so he can open his shell and close it, just like a box. *That's* why he's a box turtle. Now help me get this tub fixed up for him. Go see if Mom has a piece of lettuce and a little raw hamburger meat."

Rachel got the lettuce and meat. Wally got a shallow pan of water. "Eat your lunch," he said, putting Buddy in the tub.

But Buddy only tried to climb up the steep sides.

"He wants to get out," said Rachel. "He doesn't like it in there."

"He'll get used to it," said Wally. "Box turtles do get used to captivity."

"To what?" asked Rachel.

"Captivity. You know . . ."

But Rachel didn't know.

Wally had to explain, "They get used to being captive. To not being free."

"They do?"

"Oh sure. And I'll take good care of him. I'll give him good food, and I'll take him out for walks, so he can have sunshine and exercise."

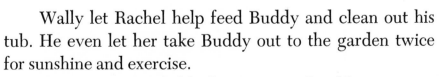

Wally let Rachel help feed Buddy and clean out his tub. He even let her take Buddy out to the garden twice for sunshine and exercise.

Even so, it wasn't like having a turtle of her own.

Every day for three days Rachel walked up the dirt
road, through the field, back to the old stone wall. "There
probably are lots more turtles here," she thought, on hands
and knees, searching all around through the grass and
weeds. When she got tired of searching, she climbed up
the wall and practiced jumping. Then she searched some
more.

The fourth day Wally came along. He stopped at some brambles and picked blackberries. Rachel went on to the wall and searched and searched—but no luck.

"Now I'll take a jumping break," she decided, and climbed up. "Get ready, on my mark, this time I'll jump really far. . . ." She sprang, saw the rock on the ground below, got frightened, twisted in the air, and landed—not on her feet, but on her left side with her arm pressed against the rock and the rest of her on top of it.

She lay there like a crooked question mark. For a long, long instant she felt nothing at all; yet, she knew for sure she was hurt.

The next instant she screamed. But the hurting grew and grew. She could not scream it away.

Then Wally was beside her. He pulled her to her feet, sat her down again against the wall, and said, "You wait here. I'll go for Mom. I'll run."

The pain in Rachel's side and upper arm got less. But below the elbow her arm hurt and hurt. It did not get better even when her mother came.

"Don't cry, darling, it'll be all right," said her mother, trying to wipe Rachel's tears away. "Dr. Shulman will take care of it, you'll see."

To Wally she said, "Stay with your sister while I get the car. I'll be right back."

She drove the car right through the field. She helped
Rachel into the front seat and gave her a pillow to rest
her arm on. Wally got in the back. The car went bump,
bump, back through the field, down the dirt road and,
despite the pillow, every bump jogged Rachel's arm.

"You'll feel better in a minute," said Dr. Shulman. "Stand still now." He turned the light off. He took an x-ray picture of her arm. He turned the light back on, went out, stayed out—more than a minute.

"I don't feel better. It hurts just as much," Rachel cried.

"I know it does," said her mother, stroking her hair. "He has to develop the x-ray and look at it, before he can do anything."

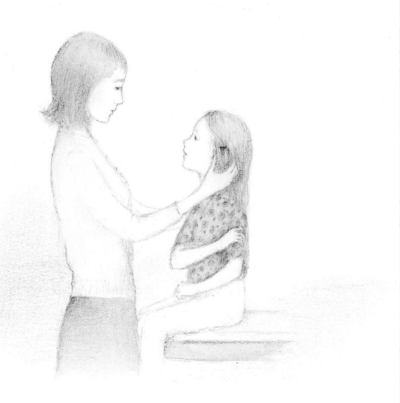

Dr. Shulman came back in. "Well, it's broken, but it's not out of place," he said.

He took Rachel's arm and, working fast, wound wet plaster bandages around and around it from just above the elbow almost down to the wrist. The plaster made them harden into a thick, round wall. This wall held Rachel's arm firmly, and kept it from having to move.

Now at last the pain let up. Rachel sighed with relief. "I've got a cast!" she said, feeling enormously proud. She remembered the morning last year when Peggy Willis had come to school with her arm in a cast. The teacher had been extra nice to her, and the whole class had made her get-well cards. Rachel almost wished it wasn't summer now, so she could go to school with her arm in a cast.

Dr. Shulman put a sling around the cast and tied it around her right shoulder. Then he switched a light on behind the dark x-ray. "Want to see the inside of your arm?" he asked, and pointed to a line going down the middle. "That's the bone. And that—" he pointed to a little gap in it—"is where the break is. Now it'll start to grow back together. Come in next Friday, and we'll see how it's doing."

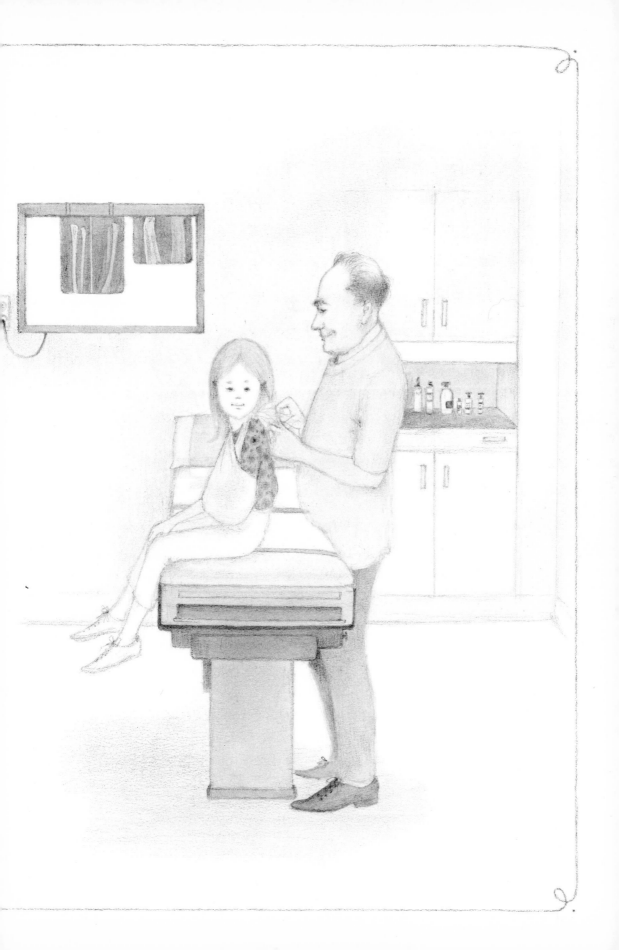

Wally had been waiting in the waiting room. "Neat!"
he said when Rachel came out. And in a hushed voice he
asked, "Is it broken?"

"Yes, it's broken," Rachel said.

"When we get home, can I write my name on your
cast?"

Rachel said he could.

Wally held the car door open for her. He let her get
in first, and gave her plenty of room. He acted as if she
were someone important, not his kid sister. "Does your
arm still hurt?" he asked.

Rachel shook her head.

"What does it feel like, having a cast?"

"Different. Hard." Rachel wondered how else to describe it when, all of a sudden, she thought of the turtle. "It feels like having a—," she started to say.

"A what?" Wally wanted to know.

But she smiled to herself and didn't tell.

While Wally was writing his name on her cast, Rachel thought some more about turtles. "Let's go down and see what Buddy's doing," she said.

Buddy was busy trying to climb out of the tub, as usual.

Wally picked him up. "Here, you hold him," he said and put him down on Rachel's sling-covered cast.

Rachel let him take a few steps up toward her elbow. She had to spread the fingers of her right hand wide to get a grip on his shell. "You know something?" she said, hoping Wally wouldn't laugh at her, and told him what she had not said in the car: "I'm sort of like a turtle now. I mean, my cast is sort of like a turtle's shell."

"You know something else?" Wally looked away. He sounded embarrassed. "You can have him. I'm giving him to you."

"You mean it?" Rachel jumped up and down, clanked her cast against the door, and nearly dropped the turtle.

"Hey, watch out," said Wally.

"Thanks," said Rachel. Now she looked away and sounded embarrassed. "Thanks a lot. You want my goldfish?"

"No, that's okay," said Wally and he went upstairs.

"You won't have to stay down here all by yourself anymore," Rachel told the turtle. "You can live in my room from now on."

She looked around the basement for something to keep him in, and saw the very thing: a deep, white enamel basin with some old mops and brooms standing in it.

She put the turtle down. "Wait right here," she said. She took the mops and brooms out of the basin and leaned them up against the wall. She found a rag and wiped the basin clean.

Now where was Buddy? He hadn't waited. He had crawled all the way across the floor. Rachel went after him. "Whoever said turtles are slow was wrong," she said and put him in the basin. With her right arm around it, she held it against her cast and struggled up the stairs, through the kitchen, through the dining room, and to the front stairs. Halfway up, she nearly dropped the basin. At last she reached her room and, with a loud clunk, put it down.

She bent to pick up Buddy.

"Tzzz," he hissed.

"Don't be scared of me, Bud—no, not Buddy. That's a boy's name. You need a turtle's name. Let's see . . ."

Rachel thought of names: Bert? Curtis? Crawly? Shelly? Theodore? No, none sounded right. So she made up a name. It was odd enough for a turtle. It sounded just like him: Quertz.

She hoped he'd like it. "Quertz, that's you, nice Quertz," she said.

She made a sign:

And she taped it on her door.

"Rachel and WHAT?" asked Wally when he saw the sign.

"Quertz. That's what I'm calling my turtle."

"Hey, you can't do that!"

"Why not?"

"Because he's used to 'Buddy.' Watch—" Wally lifted the turtle out of the basin onto the floor. The turtle started crawling toward the window. "He'll come when I call him," said Wally. "Buddy!"

The turtle did not turn around.

"Buddy! Hey, Buddy, come here!"

But the turtle continued on his way.

"He *would* have got used to 'Buddy' after a while," said Wally.

"He'll get used to 'Quertz' in a while, won't you, Quertz?" said Rachel and put him back in his basin.

In bed that night, listening to him scrabble, Rachel thought that getting Quertz was much, much better than getting a lot of get-well cards. Get-well cards couldn't make up for a broken arm. Quertz did. Maybe he even more than made up for it.

Not that it was easy, doing things with one arm. Rachel needed her mother to help her put on dresses or blouses and take them off. Just like a baby, she thought. But when she tried to push her bad arm into the sleeve hole without help she always made it hurt. Brushing her teeth or washing herself took her twice as long now. And even though she could use the fingers of her left hand a little bit, there were some perfectly easy things like tying a shoelace that she couldn't do at all. "Oh well, I'll get used to it," she decided. "Hold still now," she told Quertz. She wanted him to pose for her. She was drawing a picture of him on her cast.

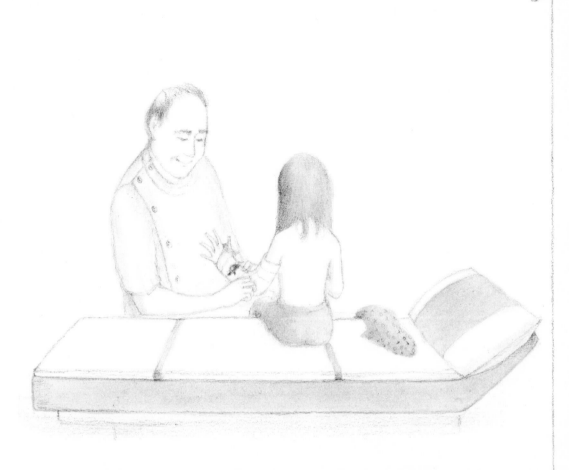

"That's a good-looking turtle," said Dr. Shulman on Friday when Rachel came for her checkup. "Is it any turtle in particular?"

"Yes, mine," said Rachel. "He's really better looking than that. I couldn't draw him too well. He wouldn't hold still."

"But *you* will, won't you?" said Dr. Shulman and took another x-ray of her arm.

"It's doing fine," he said. "In five weeks or so it'll be as good as new." And he put a clean sling on.

The second week, just when Rachel thought she was getting used to her arm in a cast, it started to itch, especially at night.

She called her mother. "It itches so much, and I can't scratch. What'll I do?"

Her mother fluffed up her pillow. "Try thinking about something else," she said. "That sometimes gets rid of an itch better than scratching."

So Rachel thought about Quertz. Did he itch too, inside his shell? She wondered, and her arm itched all the more.

In the morning she borrowed one of Wally's pet books. It had a whole chapter about turtles, but not a word about whether they itched.

Rachel asked Wally.

"I bet they don't," he said.

The third week the weather turned very hot. Rachel took Quertz to visit a friend who lived near a brook. "Look at him go!" she said, amazed at what a good, fast swimmer he was with such a heavy shell to carry. He would have swum away in a minute if she had not caught him.

"You're still not used to capt—captivity, are you? You just want to escape," she reproached him.

"Tzzz," said Quertz and pulled his head inside his shell.

On Sunday Rachel and Wally's parents took them to
a lake. The water was warm and inviting. Rachel was a
good swimmer too. But she could only go in up to her
knees. She couldn't swim with her cast on, she wasn't
allowed to get it wet.

"Three more weeks to go," said Dr. Shulman on the third Friday. Rachel was disappointed. The third week had seemed so long, more like two weeks than one.

From then on the days crept by—much more slowly than turtles.

On Wednesday of the fourth week the real Buddy came to visit Wally.

Rachel showed him Quertz.

Buddy signed his name on Rachel's cast.

"Let's go play in the field," said Wally.

"Can I come?" asked Rachel.

"Do you always have to tag along, pest?" said Wally.

"Wally!" said their mother sharply. But to Rachel she said, "I'd rather you didn't jump off that wall for a while. You'd better stay home and find something else to do."

"Oh Mom! I can't ride my bike, I can't play ball, I can't swim, I can't do anything!"

"You can help bake toll-house cookies, can't you? And later you can lick the bowl, can't you?"

But helping bake cookies and licking the bowl took less than an hour. The rest of the day seemed like a year.

All this time Rachel had been taking as good care of Quertz as when she first got him. She let him have a straw-berry every day because the pet book said berries were box turtles' favorite food; she changed his water, cleaned his

basin, and took him out for airings. But it made her sad that he still didn't come to her when she called his name, and that he still always tried to get away.

As the weeks crept on, Rachel's neck and shoulders ached from having to carry the heavy cast around. Instead of getting used to it, she hated it more all the time, and minded more and more about the many things she couldn't do.

Did being the owner of Quertz still make up for having a broken arm? She asked herself that question. And, much as she loved him, the answer was: no.

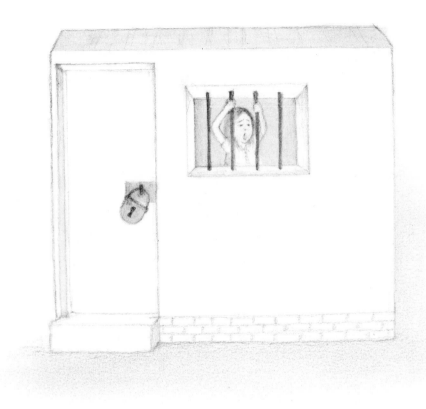

One hot sticky night, she moved his basin out of her room into the bathroom. It was hard enough trying to fall asleep with her arm so itchy and prickly inside the cast, without having to listen to his scrabbling as he tried and tried to climb out.

That night she dreamed she was shut up inside a white jail. "Let me out! Let me out!" she cried. But nobody came.

But the sixth, last, longed-for checkup came, and with a pair of sharp shears Dr. Shulman cut the cast apart, on Friday, on Freeday, and Rachel felt like shouting, my arm is free, it's free!

Dr. Shulman shook hands with it. "Good as new," he said.

Slowly Rachel bent it, stretched it out, stretched it sideways. It felt strange. "It doesn't feel like *my* arm," she said.

"Give it time," said Dr. Shulman. "It will."

It did, very soon, only better. It felt feather light and giant strong, ready to open doors, hug people, pick up pets —do anything!

"Look! No more cast!" she shouted, waving her free arm in Wally's face.

"You know something?" said Wally, half teasing, half serious, "Now you're not like Quertz anymore. You're out of your cast, but he's still in his—"

Rachel didn't wait for him to finish. She ran up the stairs two at a time. There was something Wally didn't know and the pet book didn't say, something she had almost known for a while, and now she really knew it.

Her cast had *not* been like Quertz's shell. His shell was a *part* of him. Her cast had been like the white basin-jail Quertz was in, and would never, never get used to.

She snatched him out of it and ran downstairs.

"Hey, where're you going?" Wally shouted. But Rachel was already out the door.

She ran up the dirt road, through the field, all the way to the three-sided old wall. There she set the turtle down. "Now it's your Freeday too!" she called as he crawled quickly, quickly—to a blackberry feast? to his home? to other turtles?—through brambles and weeds, away to wherever he liked.